Snow
Prune

Oxford University Press

Oxford University Press, Great Clarendon Street, Oxford OX2 6DP

Oxford   New York
Athens   Auckland   Bangkok   Bogota   Bombay
Buenos Aires   Calcutta   Cape Town   Dar es Salaam
Delhi   Florence   Hong Kong   Istanbul   Karachi
Kuala Lumpur   Madras   Madrid   Melbourne
Mexico City   Nairobi   Paris   Singapore
Taipei   Tokyo   Toronto   Warsaw

and associated companies in
Berlin   Ibadan

Oxford is a trade mark of Oxford University Press

ISBN 0 19 918574 3   School edition
ISBN 0 19 918591 3   Bookshop edition

Printed in Great Britain by Ebenezer Baylis

Illustrations by Peter Kavanagh

Photograph of Pippa Goodhart © Mouse

Chapter One

Prunella Taylor was born on the same day as her lovely Granny Prue. That was why her parents called her Prunella.

Prunella didn't like her name. She liked it even less when people called her 'Prune'. And it got worse when she moved to a new school.

Prunella was very tall.
She was the tallest in her class.
She had to look down when
she talked to the other
children. She couldn't
help it.

But the other children didn't like it.

'You're snooty!' said a girl called Beth. 'A snooty prune!' Everyone laughed. So Beth said it again.

Snooty Prune!
Snooty Prune!

Then they all said it.

Snooty Prune! Snooty Prune!

For days and weeks they went on.
They used it as her name all the time.

Prunella hated it. And she hated the
children at school for using it. Most of
all she hated Beth. But she didn't want
to hate people. What she really wanted
was a friend. Prunella wished very
hard for a friend.

One day the doorbell rang.

Chapter Two

It was Mrs Farey at the door. Mrs Farey lived over the road. She was interesting. She wore strange clothes and kept ducks and cats. Prunella liked her.

Hello, my dear. I have something for you. A small present to say thank you for feeding my cats last week.

Finger by finger, Mrs Farey opened out her hand to show a tiny parcel.

'It's very little,' she said. 'But I hope that it will bring you your biggest wish!'

'Thank you!' said Prunella.

'That's all right, my dear,' said Mrs Farey. 'Happy day!'

Prunella looked at the tiny parcel. It was very thin and wrapped in paper the colour of cats' eyes.

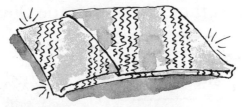

She pulled the parcel gently open. Inside was a tiny red book of stamps.

'What a strange present!' said her mother. But Prunella knew that the stamps were a wonderful present.

Those tiny bits of sticky paper would let you send messages to anyone in the world. With a stamp you could write to the Prime Minister or the Queen.

How lovely! A letter from Prunella!

You could send off for things.

Or you could send a sneaky letter to school to tell them that Beth Hall was a bully. But Prunella didn't want to sneak on Beth.

What she really wanted to do was to write to a friend. A friend would write back. If only she had a friend.

Prunella stood up and something fell to the floor.

It was a small, folded bit of newspaper. It had been put into the parcel with the stamps.

Prunella opened it out and read –

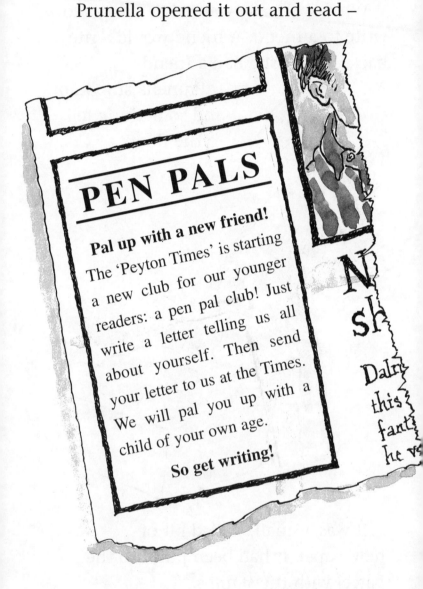

PEN PALS

Pal up with a new friend!
The 'Peyton Times' is starting a new club for our younger readers: a pen pal club! Just write a letter telling us all about yourself. Then send your letter to us at the Times. We will pal you up with a child of your own age.

So get writing!

N
Sh
Dal
this
fant
he v

I will, thought Prunella. I'll make
a pen pal friend!
Oh, thank
you, Mrs Farey!

She got out paper and
a pen and sat
down to write.

Chapter Three

Fern Lea
Lynmouth Road
Peyton
24th March

Dear Pen Pal,
        my name is Prunella.
I am tall and have long straight
hair. I haven't got any brothers
or sisters. Have you? I used
to have a goldfish but it died.
Have you got any pets?

Then she chewed her pen and frowned. She looked at the letter. It was boring.

If she had got that letter, she wouldn't want to be pen pals with the person who wrote it.

She scrumpled it up and threw it in the bin. Then she started again on a new bit of paper.

Fern Lea
Lynmouth Road
Peyton
24th March

Dear Pen Pal,
        my name is Penny.
I am quite short and I have
black curly hair. I play the
violin. Here is a picture
of me.

2.

I have an older sister called Serena who is very beautiful. Lots of boys are in love with her, but she would rather be with me. She plaits ribbons into my hair and explains things to me.

I also have a tiny baby brother called Leo. I found him. If you want to know how I found him, then you will have to write to me and ask. Then I will tell you.

3.

I also have a big soppy dog called Nelly and three sweet kittens called Button, Zip and Velcro.

I have lots of friends at school. But I would like you to be my friend too because I like getting letters. Please write to me very soon.

Your friend,
Penny.

Prunella made the 'Y' of Penny swirl under the rest of the name.

She put the letter into an envelope
addressed to the Peyton Times.

Then she tore out the first of Mrs
Farey's stamps. She held it between a
finger and thumb and closed her eyes.
She wished hard. Please bring me a
pen pal who will be a real friend!

She stuck on the stamp and
ran all the way to
the post box.

A reply came four
days later. It was
addressed to
Miss P Taylor.

19

There's a letter for you. It's got a local post mark. Who can that be from?
I expect it's from a friend, Dad.

She opened it in her room and read:

20 Ring Road
Peyton
27th March

Dear Penny,
        I like your letter very much and I would like to be your pen pal. Please write and tell me how you found Leo.
        I had better tell you about myself. My name is Angel. I haven't got any brothers or sisters. I haven't got a mother or a father either. I am an orphan. My father died before I was born.

2.

He was an explorer. One day in the Antarctic he met a polar bear. They had a fight.

My father and the bear killed each other. But before my father died, he wrote something in the snow. He didn't have a pen or anything. He wrote with his own _blood_!

3.

He drew a big heart and wrote "Alesha + Baby" inside the heart.

Alesha + Baby

Alesha was my mother and I was the baby. At least I know that my father loved me. Even though he never met me.

My mother died when I was born. She looked at me in the nurse's arms. With her last breath she said "Poor little angel." That is how I got my name.

4.

Here is a picture of what I looked like then and what I look like now.

Poor little angel...

Write soon and tell me about Leo.
Lots of love from
Angel

The address at the top of Angel's letter was 20, Ring Road, Peyton. Prunella had never noticed an orphanage on the Ring Road.

Perhaps Angel lived all by herself? Or maybe she had been adopted? I'll write and ask her, she thought.

Chapter Four

Fern Lea
Lynmouth Road
Peyton
28th March

Dear Angel,

Thank you for your letter. I've never known an orphan before. Who do you live with now? Are they nice to you?

Here is how I found my baby brother. At Christmas Serena took me and Nelly the dog to London to see the Christmas lights.

Wow!

2.

We went to Trafalgar Square to see the big Christmas tree. It was getting late and it was very dark. Then I heard a strange noise. "It must be the pigeons," said Serena. But it wasn't.

Nelly and I went to find out what was making the noise. Nelly sniffed and I listened. The noise and smell came from one of those great big lions. I thought that the lion had come alive!

3.

Then I saw that there was something white between his paws. It was a tiny baby wrapped in a blanket.

We took the baby to the police. Did you know that if you find something and nobody claims it, then you can keep it?

4.

Well, nobody claimed the baby.
Serena and I asked Mum if we
could have him. Mum said,
"Of course!" so we kept him.
We call him Leo because he was
found on a lion.

Write soon and tell me about
being an orphan.

Love from your friend,

Penny

P.S. You look very beautiful.

Angel's reply came in a dirty old
envelope.

It said:

20 Ring Road
Peyton
29th March

Dear Penny,

You have guessed my dark secret! I live with my Aunt Nag. She is very old and very ugly and very cruel.

← whip

I have to live in the attic. It has a hard bed and nothing else in it. I live like a slave. Aunt Nag makes me work all day long. I only get leftovers to eat. My attic is freezing cold.

My only friend is a little robin.
He comes to the window each morning.
When I read "Dear Angel" and
"love from your friend Penny" it warms
my heart. At least I know that
you love me. The picture that I drew
of me was a lie. I am really very
skinny and dressed in rags.

← robin

Lots and lots of love from your
hungry friend,
Angel

Prunella was horrified and excited by
that letter. She wrote a quick reply.

Fern Lea
Lynmouth Road
Peyton
30th March

Dear Angel,
        Here are all my sweets.
They will stop you from starving. I
have to go to school today but
tomorrow I will rescue you. Please wear
your fringe in a pony-tail. Nobody
else does that. That way, I will be
sure to know that you are you.
        I'll see you soon!
        Love from your friend
                Penny

Prunella posted the letter on her way
to school.

Chapter Five

Prunella woke very early on Saturday morning. She felt sure that Aunt Nag would lie in bed for hours. It would be best to rescue Angel while Aunt Nag was still in bed.

Then I'll bring her home, thought Prunella. Mum and Dad have always wanted another child. Angel can be my new sister as well as my friend!

Angel would find out that Penny was really Prunella. But Prunella wasn't worried. After all, Angel had pretended to be something different too. Angel had pretended to be pink and pretty.
Really she was starving and skinny.

Still, Angel was expecting short dark Penny. If tall fair Prunella turned up, she had better be able to prove that she was the same person.

Prunella pulled her fringe together and tied it into a pony-tail.

Then
she
crept
downstairs
and
wrote
a
note
for
her
parents.

CRUNCH POPS

Gone out.
Back soon
with a
surprise.
Love P

With luck, she might be back before
they got up.

Outside was still dark and it was raining. The street lights looked like a row of giant sparklers along the road. It felt magical and exciting. Prunella skipped a few steps and then ran. She ran all the way to the Ring Road.

Then she slowed down. She looked at house numbers until she came to number twenty.

Number twenty wasn't the kind of house she had expected. It was a very ordinary house. Nobody would ever guess that there was a poor orphan trapped inside. Prunella looked up.

There was a light on in the attic. That must be where Angel lived.

Prunella pulled her wet fringe pony-tail straight. Then she pushed the door bell.

DING DONG!

A dog woofed from inside. Prunella could see the dog in her mind. It was a huge dog with big yellow teeth. Aunt Nag loved the dog but hated Angel.

WOOF!

Aunt Nag fed the dog proper food. Angel only got scraps.
   Poor Angel.

PRINCE

Prunella rang the bell again, long
and loud.

ING DONG DING DONG DING DONG

A light went on and there were
footsteps. The door opened and
Prunella gasped.

There stood Beth Hall with a mouth
full of sweets.

Er! I think I've got the wrong house.

But Beth had her fringe
in a pony-tail.

Behind Beth came Beth's
mother, two brothers
and a small dog.

Beth was staring at Prunella's fringe.

41

Beth's room was in the attic but it wasn't bare or cold. It was warm and it was full of mess. There were two beds by the wall. One of them had a lump in it.

'That's my stupid little sister,' said Beth.

'But Angel was an orphan! She didn't even have any brothers or sisters!' said Prunella. 'You lied!'

'Well you made up Penny too!' said Beth. 'Why did you do that?'

'That's different,' said Prunella. 'I had to make things up because nobody likes real me.

'I wish I was short and had brothers and sisters. I wish I wasn't called Prunella. I wish I had a proper name like everyone else! You're like that already. Why did you make up Angel?'

Beth's little sister popped her head out from her duvet.

Who's Angel and who's Penny?

'Nobody!' said Prunella.
'Mind your own business!' said Beth.
Beth's little sister sat right up in bed.

Why have you both got your hair in that stupid way? Are you friends?

'Maybe,' said Beth.

'Can I have one of those sweets?' asked her little sister.

'Yes,' said Prunella.

Thanks. Can I say something else? If you don't like being called Prunella, why don't you just be Ella? Ella's a nice name.

Prunella thought for a moment.
'That's a good idea,' she said. 'I like
Ella.'

'So do I,' said Beth Hall. 'Let's really
be friends.'

About the author

I live in Leicester with my
husband, my three young
daughters, a big dog and
a small cat. When I'm
not busy being a mum,
I am an author. One of
the nice things about
being an author is all

the post that you send and receive.
I'm always excited when I see the postman
coming down the road. He might bring a
letter from a friend or, if I'm very lucky, he
might bring a parcel full of books made out
of one of my stories. Those are my favourite
kinds of post to open! What are yours?

Other Treetops books at this level include:
Shelley Holmes, Ace Detective by Michaela Morgan
Here Comes Trouble by Tessa Krailing
Cool Clive and the Little Pest by Michaela Morgan
Pass the Ball, Grandad by Debbie White
The Terrible Birthday Present by Angela Bull

Also available in packs
Stage 12 pack C   0 19 918577 8
Stage 12 class pack C   0 19 918578 6